Secret PRINCESSES

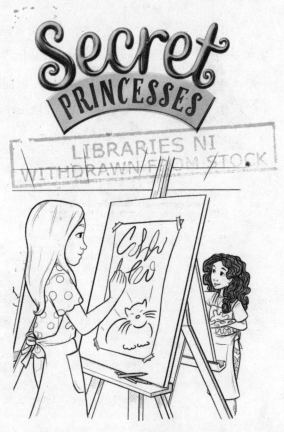

Picture Perfect

ROSIE BANKS

Wishing Star Palace

The Secret Princess Promise

"I promise that I will be kind and brave,

Using my magic to help and save,

Granting wishes and doing my best,

To make people smile and bring happiness."

# CONTENTS

CHAPTER ONE

A Birthday Surprise

"Can you tie this please, Dad?" asked
Charlotte Williams, handing her father the
blue balloon she'd just blown up. As her dad
tied a knot, Charlotte puffed into a yellow
balloon. Blue and yellow were her little
brothers' favourite colours.

"I think that's plenty," Charlotte's dad
said, sticking balloons around the arched

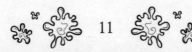

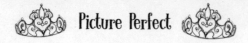

doorway that led from the hallway into the kitchen. Next, they stretched a banner reading *Happy Birthday* across the hall.

"The twins are going to be so surprised," Charlotte said, gazing at the decorations with satisfaction.

"I hope so!" said Dad, ruffling her brown curls.

Harvey and Liam had had their birthday party the previous weekend. They had gone go-karting, then

 12

shared a giant pizza with all their friends.
But today was their actual birthday.
Charlotte's mum had taken the twins to the
beach, so that Charlotte and her dad could
decorate the house and surprise the boys.

"It's still so weird that it's warm enough
to go to the beach on their birthday,"
Charlotte said.

When their family lived in England, the
twins' birthday party was always indoors
because it was too cold to play outside.
Since moving to sunny California, however,
they could go to the beach all year round!

"Sometimes I miss the British weather,"
Dad told Charlotte, getting out a roll of
wrapping paper.

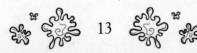

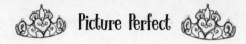

"Really?" asked Charlotte. She loved being able to be outside all the time. But she did miss playing with her best friend, Mia, who lived in England.

"How on earth am I going to wrap these?" Dad asked, holding up two leather baseball gloves.

"I'll help," Charlotte said. The gloves had the logo of the twins' favourite baseball team on them.

Back in England, Charlotte's brothers had been obsessed with football. They still loved to play football, though they called it soccer now. But American baseball had become their new favourite game.

"Right," said Dad, as Charlotte stuck

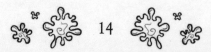

a bow on each boy's present. "Time to decorate the cake." A freshly baked chocolate cake was cooling on the kitchen counter.

"Mmm, it smells delicious," said Charlotte, breathing in the yummy chocolatey aroma.

"Hopefully I can make it look good too," Dad said, chuckling as he started icing the cake.

"I'm going to make their cards," Charlotte said. She got out a plastic box filled with arts and crafts materials and folded two pieces of white card in half. *Hmm*, Charlotte thought, drumming her pencil on the table as she tried to think of an idea.

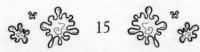

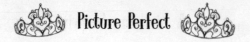

She wished Mia was there. Mia loved doing crafts – she would probably have loads of cool ideas. One year, Mia had made her a pop-up birthday card shaped like a cake!

Charlotte decided to draw a character from Liam and Harvey's favourite space movie on each card. As she sketched, she wondered when she'd see Mia again. Even though they lived thousands of miles apart now, Charlotte and Mia still saw each other – because they were training to become Secret Princesses!

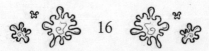

Being trainee princesses meant Charlotte and Mia got to wear beautiful tiaras and visit an amazing palace. But they got to do something much, much cooler than that, too. They made people's wishes come true using magic!

"Hey, Dad," Charlotte called out as she wrote a funny caption inside the cards. "What do you always get on your birthday?"

He looked up from the cake. "A present?"

"No," said Charlotte, giggling. "Another year older!"

Her dad's brown eyes – which were exactly same colour as Charlotte's – danced with amusement as he laughed. "Good one!

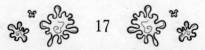

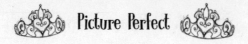

What do you think of the cake?"

Charlotte went over to take a closer look. Dad had decorated the cake with stars and planets, and topped it with a rocket. "It looks great, Dad. Ready for blast-off!"

"I wish I could make a flying cake," Dad chuckled. "The boys would love that!"

Charlotte couldn't tell her dad, but she knew a place where flying cakes did exist.

At Wishing Star Palace, Princess Sylvie baked magical cakes that could change flavour – and even fly! Charlotte suddenly longed to see Mia and all her Secret Princess friends.

She peeked down to look at her necklace. It was glowing! She stifled a gasp.

"Er, Dad," she said. "I'm going to see if I can find an envelope."

"OK," he said, sticking candles on the cake.

Charlotte raced to her bedroom. Shutting the door behind her, she eagerly looked in the mirror. Her necklace was gold with a pendant shaped like half a heart – and it was shining with magical light!

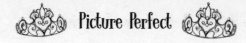

Charlotte gripped her glowing pendant tightly and said, "I wish I could see Mia!"

The light shining from the pendant grew brighter and swirled around Charlotte. *SWOOSH!* Magic swept her to Wishing Star Palace.

Looking down, Charlotte saw that her shorts and trainers had transformed into her pretty pink princess dress and sparkling red slippers. She was so excited she did a little jig on the spot in the grand entrance hall!

POOF! A girl in a gold dress and ruby slippers suddenly appeared. The diamond tiara resting on her long, blonde hair was identical to the one Charlotte was wearing. "Hi, Charlotte!" she cried, her blue eyes

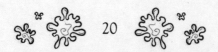

sparkling with excitement.

"Mia!" Charlotte squealed. She ran over
and hugged her best friend.

"Isn't today Liam and Harvey's birthday?"
Mia asked her.

"Yup," said Charlotte. "I was just making
their cards. I could have used your help!"

Charlotte wasn't worried about missing
her brothers' surprise. No time would pass
back in the real world while she was having
an adventure with Mia. But where were the
Secret Princesses?

AAAACHOOO!

"What was that?" Mia asked.

"I think it's someone sneezing," said
Charlotte.

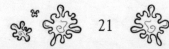

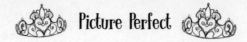

AAAACHOOO! AAAACHOOO!

Following the sound of sneezing and coughing, Charlotte and Mia arrived outside a closed door.

"I wonder who's inside?" Mia said.

"I don't know," said Charlotte. "But they don't sound well at all."

AAACCHOOO!

AAAACHOOO!
AAAACHOOO!

CHAPTER TWO
A Poorly Princess

Charlotte and Mia knocked on the door.
"Come in!" called out a muffled voice. The
girls stepped into a beautiful bedroom.
Princess Anna lay in a bed covered with a
lilac-coloured canopy. She was propped up
with pillows and her neat bun was untidier
than usual. Her face looked pale, but her
nose was bright red.

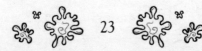

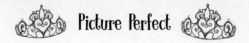

"Oh no!" cried Mia. "You poor thing!"

Princess Anna smiled weakly at her visitors. "Id's lubbly do see oo, girls," she said, sounding stuffed up.

"It's lovely to see you, too," said Mia.

"I'm sorry you're not feeling well," said Charlotte.

"I dink id's a cod," sniffled Princess Anna.

"Maybe you caught it at school," said Mia. "Lots of kids in my class have been off sick with colds."

Back in the real world, Anna was a teacher. Her necklace's pendant was shaped like an owl, showing that she was very wise.

A princess with cool red streaks in her strawberry blonde hair hugged the girls.

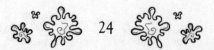

It was their old friend, Princess Alice.

"Thanks for coming, girls," she said.

"Can't you make Anna's cold go away with magic?" Charlotte asked her.

"I'm afraid not," said Alice, shaking her head.

"But we're doing everything we can to make Anna comfortable," said Princess Ella.

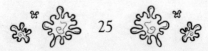

She placed an adorable white kitten gently on Anna's lap. Anna stroked the purring kitten and smiled.

Princess Evie burst into the room, holding a vase of flowers. "I picked these in the garden," she said, setting the bouquet down on Princess Anna's bedside table.

Princess Anna plucked a petal off one of the flowers and it magically turned into a silk hankie! She held it to her nose and let out a big sneeze.

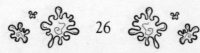

AAACCHOOOOOO!

Startled, the kitten looked up and everyone – including Anna – burst out laughing.

"Hey," said Charlotte. "I know what will cheer you up – what kind of flowers grow on your face?"

The princesses shook their heads, baffled.

"Tulips," said Charlotte, grinning. "Get it? Two lips."

Princess Anna chuckled.

Alice gently squeezed Charlotte's shoulder. "I knew I could count on you to make Anna smile."

"Yoo hoo!" said Princess Sylvie, coming into the bedroom holding a steaming mug.

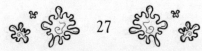

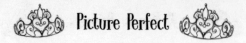

She handed it to Anna. "Here's something to soothe your throat."

"It smells delicious," said Anna, lifting the mug up and inhaling the sweet scent. "What's in it?"

"Honey, lemon and a bit of magic," said Sylvie, winking.

Mia was staring at a painting on the bedroom wall. It showed Wishing Star Palace's garden in the spring. She pointed to the bottom of the painting, where 'Princess Sophie' was written in loopy writing.

Charlotte felt a pang of worry as she remembered why Princess Sophie wasn't at Anna's bedside. It was all because of

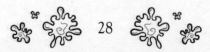

Princess Poison, who had once been a Secret Princess but now spoiled wishes instead of granting them. She had cursed four princesses' portraits and made them forget that they were Secret Princesses.

Charlotte gave Mia's hand a reassuring squeeze. "We broke the spell on Cara,

 Sylvie and Kiko," she said. "We'll break the curse on Sophie too." The only way they could do that was to show Sophie that magic was real and persuade her to return to Wishing Star Palace.

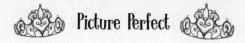

Mia nodded, her blue eyes solemn. "I know we will."

There was a knock on the bedroom door and a princess with dark curly hair and a round, freckled face came in holding a black doctor's bag. She was wearing a white coat and a stethoscope over a purple gown.

"Maria!" cried Alice. "I'm so pleased you came!"

"Of course I did," said the princess, perching on the edge of Anna's bed.

Princess Maria rummaged in her black bag and took out something that looked like a wooden lolly stick. "Can I take a peek, Anna?" she asked.

Anna nodded.

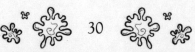

"Open wide and say 'ah'," Maria instructed her. She placed the wooden stick on Anna's tongue and peered down her throat with a little torch.

"Poor you," she said. "Your throat looks very sore."

Next, Maria popped a thermometer in Princess Anna's mouth. "You don't have a fever," she said, studying the temperature.

Maria put the ends of the stethoscope into her ears. "Take three deep breaths for me," she told Anna, gently placing the round end of the stethoscope on her patient's chest. When she'd finished examining Anna, Maria took off her stethoscope and packed it in her bag. "It's a bad cold,"

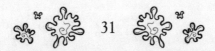

she said, patting Anna's hand. "The best thing you can do is rest."

"We'd better leave you in peace," said Alice, plumping up Anna's pillows and tucking the covers around her.

"I'll take this little guy so he doesn't bother you," Ella said, picking up the kitten.

"I hope you feel better soon," said Mia, blowing Anna a kiss.

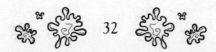

"It's so good to see you, Maria," said Ella, hugging her friend.

"I don't think you've met Mia and Charlotte yet," said Alice, leading the girls over to Maria.

"Ah! The two new trainees!" exclaimed Maria. "It's wonderful to finally meet you."

"Are you a doctor?" Charlotte asked Maria. All of the Secret Princesses had jobs in the real world – Ella was a vet, Sylvie was a baker, and Alice was a pop star!

"Yes," Maria said. "I've been so busy studying for exams that I haven't been able to come to the palace much lately."

"Why do you need to take exams if you're already a doctor?" Mia asked her.

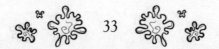

"Doctors sometimes study to become specialists," explained Maria. "Medical training has lots of different stages."

"Just like training to become a Secret Princess," said Mia.

"That's right," said Maria, smiling. Touching the diamond tiara on Charlotte's head, she said, "I can see that you both passed the first stage of your training."

"And the second," said Mia, showing Maria her ruby slippers.

"We only need one more sapphire to get our princess rings," said Charlotte, showing Maria the three blue jewels in her necklace's pendant. She and Mia had earned them by granting three wishes.

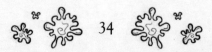

"After you've earned your rings, you'll be working towards getting your moonstone bracelet," said Maria, holding out her wrist to show them a delicate gold bangle with a cloudy white gem. "It's how I knew that Princess Anna was unwell. The moonstone lets you talk to other princesses." She tapped the gem on the bracelet and said, "Princess Anna." Immediately Princess Anna's moonstone began to glow. When she tapped it, she and Maria could talk to each other. "It's a bit

like a walkie talkie," Maria explained. "Just more magical!"

"Cool!" said Charlotte.

Light began to shine around the room, but it wasn't coming from the princesses' moonstone bracelets, or from their sapphire rings, which flashed when danger was near. Their wands were glowing!

"A wish needs granting!" cried Mia.

"Can we go?" asked Charlotte. "Please?"

"Of course," said Alice.

"Good luck," said Maria.

"Let's use our ruby slippers," said Charlotte, eager to get started quickly.

Mia and Charlotte clicked the heels of their ruby slippers together three times and said, "The Mirror Room."

Magic carried them to a small room at the top of one of the palace's four towers. The only thing in the room was an oval mirror in a gold frame. Reflected on the glass was the image of a girl with brown hair in two French plaits. She was wearing an apron that said *Smart Arts* and looked worried.

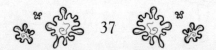

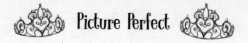
"So that's whose wish we need to grant,"
said Mia, nudging Charlotte.

Fancy writing appeared on the mirror and
Charlotte read the words out loud:

**"A wish needs granting, adventures await,
Call Isla's name, don't hesitate!"**

"Isla!" Mia and Charlotte said together.
The mirror's surface churned with light.

"Ready?" Charlotte asked Mia.

Mia nodded and they both touched
the mirror. Charlotte's heart raced as the
light pulled them away from the palace. If
they granted Isla's wish, they'd earn their
sapphire rings!

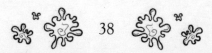

CHAPTER THREE
Smart Arts

The magic whisked them to a busy high street lined with shops. Because of the magic, none of the shoppers noticed Mia and Charlotte appear out of thin air. The girls didn't look out of place, because their princess dresses had magically changed into jeans and T-shirts.

"How are we ever going to find Isla?"

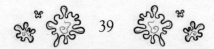

Charlotte wondered, looking up and down the street.

"She's in there," said Mia, pointing to a shop with a red awning and a sign that said *Smart Arts*.

"How do you know?" asked Charlotte.

"Because that's what it said on her apron," Mia said.

"Of course," said Charlotte. "Well done, Detective Mia!"

"Let's go and meet her," said Mia, linking arms with Charlotte.

They hurried down the pavement, arm in arm, and went into Smart Arts. When the bell above the door tinkled, the girl behind the till looked up. It was Isla!

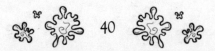

"Welcome to Smart Arts," she said, smiling. "Can I help you find something?"

"No thanks," said Charlotte. "We're just, er, browsing."

Isla looked disappointed. "Well, let me know if you need any help."

Charlotte and Mia wandered down an

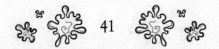

aisle full of all kinds of art supplies – from oil paints and paintbrushes to pencils and pastels. Another aisle had craft materials, its shelves heaving with glitter and glue, crayons and clay, stickers and scissors. There was thick paper in every shade of the rainbow.

"This stuff would have been handy when I was making the twins' birthday cards," said Charlotte.

At the back of the shop were easels for customers to try out different paints and brushes. There was a noticeboard covered with fliers advertising local art classes and exhibitions. A tabby cat was napping on top of a bookcase crammed full of art books.

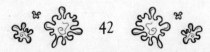

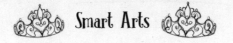

"Wow," said Mia, stroking the cat. "Craft supplies and cats. This shop is perfect."

"So why do you suppose Isla looked so worried?" Charlotte asked.

The cat stretched, jumped down from the bookcase and padded down the aisle.

"I'm not sure," Mia said. "But let's try to find out." They followed the cat to the till, where Isla was folding white paper.

"What are you making?" Charlotte asked.

"A swan," said Isla, holding up a paper bird. "I do origami when the shop isn't busy." She sighed and gestured to a whole shelf full of origami birds. "As you can see, we aren't very busy most of the time."

"I'm surprised to hear that," said Mia.

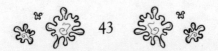

"This is a great shop."

"Thanks," said Isla. "I'm Isla, by the way. Isla Smart."

"As in Smart Arts?" asked Charlotte.

"That's right," said Isla, smiling. "This is my mum's shop. She's working in the back office right now."

"I'm Charlotte," said Charlotte. "And this is my friend Mia."

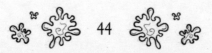

44

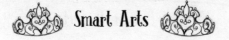

"Who's this gorgeous guy?" asked Mia, stooping to stroke the tabby cat.

"That's Picasso," said Isla. She bent down and when she straightened up she was holding a black and white cat. "And this is Matisse."

"Those are funny names," said Charlotte.

"They're named after my mum's two favourite artists," explained Isla.

"Your mum must really love art," said Mia, with a giggle.

"She does," said Isla, setting Matisse down on the counter. "She used all of her savings to open this shop a few months ago, but if we don't get more customers it won't stay open much longer."

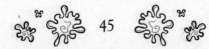

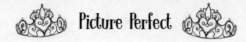

"I'm sorry to hear that," said Charlotte.

"Mum's worked so hard," Isla said sadly.
"I don't want the shop to shut down. I really
wish it could be a success."

Charlotte nudged Mia with her elbow.
They had discovered Isla's wish!

"Maybe people don't know about the shop
yet," said Mia.

"Yes," agreed Charlotte. "You need to
spread the word."

"Mum doesn't have any money to
advertise," said Isla.

Charlotte suddenly remembered
something she'd seen earlier. "I've got an
idea!" She dashed to the back of the shop
and scanned the noticeboard until she

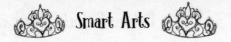
found what she was looking for.

"There's an Open Day," Charlotte said, running back with the flier. "It's happening at somewhere called The Old Warehouse today. It says you can visit artists' studios and watch them working."

"Is that near here?" Mia asked Isla.

"Yes," said Isla. "It's really close. But how does that help?"

"You can tell the artists there about the shop," explained Charlotte. "Hopefully they'll come and buy all their art supplies here."

"I can't leave the shop," said Isla sadly. "I'm supposed to be looking after the till while Mum works in the office."

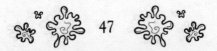

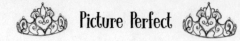

"We can go," Charlotte volunteered.

"We can make leaflets to hand out to the artists," said Mia.

"That would be amazing," said Isla, her face lighting up.

"Maybe you could have a special one-day sale," Charlotte suggested. "That might get more people to come."

"Let me just check with Mum," said Isla, coming around the counter. Hurrying to the back of the shop, she disappeared behind a little red door.

A moment later she returned, beaming. "Mum thinks it's a great idea. She says we can use whatever supplies we need to make the adverts."

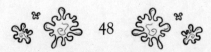

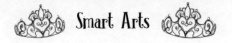

Isla, Mia and Charlotte went over to the easels. Putting on aprons, they painted fliers advertising Smart Arts' One-Day Sale.

Mia drew a picture of a cat and wrote "The Purr-fect Place to Buy Art Supplies" on her fliers.

On Charlotte's adverts, she painted a rainbow with the caption "Get Every Colour of the Rainbow at Smart Arts."

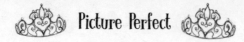

The front door bell jingled and Isla put down her paintbrush. "There's a customer!" she said excitedly. "I'd better see if they need help."

"Hopefully they'll buy lots and lots!" Charlotte said.

As the girls continued to paint adverts, they could hear Isla speaking to the customer in the paint aisle. "What colour spray paint are you looking for?" Isla asked.

"Green," said a man.

Charlotte frowned. The man's voice sounded very familiar.

"Here you go," said Isla. "Is there anything else I can help you with?"

"Yes," said the man rudely. "You can get

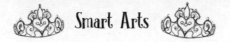
out of my way!"

Alarmed, Charlotte realised why she recognised the man's voice – it was Princess Poison's mean servant! "It's Hex!" she said to Mia.

The girls ran to the paint aisle just in time to see a short, tubby man push past Isla and run out of the shop.

"He's stealing a can of spray paint!" cried Isla.

"We'll stop him!" said Charlotte, sprinting after Hex. She and Mia raced out of the shop. Hex hadn't gone far – he was standing in front of the shop, a nasty grin on his face.

"Give that back!" Mia demanded angrily.

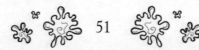

"You need a new policy in this shop – try before you buy," said Hex. Shaking the can, he yanked off the cap and tossed it on the ground. As Mia and Charlotte stared in horror, he sprayed huge, green letters on the shop window.

"Nope," said Hex, throwing the spray paint away. "I'm not going to buy it after all." He went off, laughing.

Isla ran out of the shop. "Did you catch him?" Then, noticing the window, she gasped as she read the words Hex had written:

THIS SHOP IS RUBBISH!

CHAPTER FOUR

Sophie's Studio

Tears filled Isla's eyes as she stared at Hex's rude graffiti. "Why would he do that?" she wailed.

Mia and Charlotte exchanged glances. They knew exactly why Hex had done it – he was trying to spoil Isla's wish!

Charlotte quickly tried to wipe the spray paint off the glass but it was just no use.

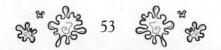

The green paint wouldn't rub off.

"Those fliers we made were a complete waste. Nobody will want to come into the shop now," said Isla.

"Don't worry," Mia said. "We can fix this."

"How?" asked Isla. "It will take ages to scrub the paint off."

"Not if we use magic," Charlotte said, her eyes sparkling. It was time to make a wish!

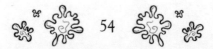

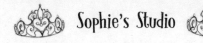

She and Mia held their glowing pendants together, forming a perfect heart. "I wish for the shop window to look lovely," Charlotte said.

There was a flash of light and Hex's ugly graffiti was replaced by a beautifully painted scene. Pink and pale blue candyfloss blossomed on bushes, scarlet candy apples grew on trees, and brightly coloured lollipops sprouted from green grass. It was the perfect way to advertise the art shop – with some beautiful art!

Mia murmured, "That looks just like the—"

"Wishing Star Palace garden," Charlotte finished for her.

Isla looked at the window, amazed. "It's gorgeous," she said. "How did you do that?"

"It was magic, like we said," Charlotte told her.

"How can you do magic?" Isla asked, still looking bewildered.

"We're training to become Secret Princesses," explained Mia. "We help grant people's wishes using our magic necklaces."

"You wished for your mum's shop to be a success, didn't you?" added Charlotte.

"So we're going to do everything we can to make that happen."

"Me too," said Isla. She picked up the can of spray paint Hex had dropped and added a finishing touch to the beautiful window art. "SALE ON NOW!" she wrote in cute bubble letters on the glass.

The window was already attracting attention. Shoppers walking down the street stopped to admire the scene and peer inside.

"Let's go back in," Mia said. "You don't want to miss any customers."

When they went back into the shop, Isla's mum came out of the back room. She was wearing dungarees, pink canvas trainers and dangly earrings. A bandana

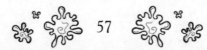

was holding back her hair, which the same
reddish-brown colour as Isla's.

"Did I hear
a customer,
sweetheart?" she
asked.

"Yes, but he didn't
buy anything," Isla
said, truthfully.

"Never mind," Isla's
mum said, giving her
daughter a quick hug.
"Perhaps he'll come

back and buy something another time."
Although she was trying to sound positive,
Isla's mum's forehead creased with worry.

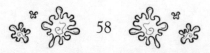

"We'd better go and deliver the adverts to the Old Warehouse," Charlotte said.

"That's so kind of you," Isla's mum said. "We really appreciate it."

Once they'd gathered up all the adverts, Mia asked, "How do we get there?"

"Turn left down the high street. It's the old brick building at the end," Isla's mum said. "You can't miss it."

Mia and Charlotte followed the directions and soon arrived at the Old Warehouse. A big banner saying *Open Day* hung over the entrance. Inside, the big building had been divided into small studios where artists were busy making and selling their work.

The girls went into a studio where a man

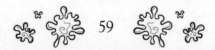

was shaping wet clay into a bowl on a
pottery wheel.

"Smart Arts is having a sale today,"
Charlotte told the potter. "It's only a few
minutes from here."

"That's good to know," said the potter.
He wiped his hands on his apron and took a
flier from Mia.

Next, they went into a studio where a
lady was making jewellery. Her necklaces
and earrings had bold, funky designs.

"Smart Arts sells beads," Charlotte
informed her.

"Everything is ten percent off today," Mia
added shyly, giving her a flier.

"Cool," said the lady, tucking the advert

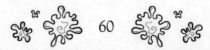

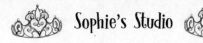

into her pocket. "I'll check it out."

Soon they had given leaflets to every studio on the ground floor.

"Do you think the artists will actually go to the shop?" Mia asked Charlotte as they climbed the stairs to the next floor.

"I really hope so," Charlotte said. Their magic wasn't powerful enough to simply grant Isla's wish, so they had to hope that their plan worked.

The girls darted in and out of studios, giving adverts to painters, sculptors and artisans. Finally, they only had one left.

"We haven't been in there yet," said Mia, pointing to a large studio space at the end of the hallway.

They went into the studio and saw a lady
with brown hair standing at an easel. When
she turned around, Charlotte gasped. It was
Princess Sophie!

"Is this your studio?" Mia asked her.

"Yes, it is," Sophie said, greeting them
with a smile. "Hi, I'm Sophie."

"We know," said Charlotte. "We've met you at Wishing Star Palace."

Sophie laughed. "I think you're mixing me up with someone else. I'm just a painter."

"No you're not," Mia insisted. "You're also a Secret Princess who can do magic and grant wishes!"

As Sophie unscrewed the cap on a tube of paint, Charlotte noticed the sapphire on her ring. "Your ring is flashing!" she cried. "Danger is near!"

"Oh, that's just the light," Sophie said, glancing up at the skylight. "I'm glad it's sunny because I have to finish a special portrait today."

"Who are you painting?" Mia asked.

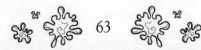

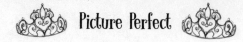

"Me," came an icy voice behind them.

Charlotte's heart sank. Turning around, she saw Princess Poison stride into the studio. She was wearing a green dress with pointy shoulders. She was with a girl who had short, dark hair – her trainee, Jinx.

"I can't wait to see my portrait," Princess Poison said.

"It's nearly done," Sophie said. "Let me fetch it." She disappeared into the back of her studio, where canvases were stacked against the wall.

"We've got to warn her," Mia said to Charlotte, dragging her over to Sophie.

"This lady is dangerous," Charlotte whispered. "That's why your sapphire

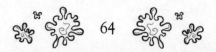

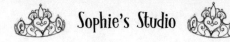
ring was flashing just now."

"Don't be silly," said Sophie, rummaging through her canvases. "She owns an art gallery called the Hexagon, and displayed my work there."

"It's all just a trick!" said Mia. "She only displayed your portraits so she could curse four Secret Princesses."

"Are those girls bothering you?" called Princess Poison.

"They're just confused," said Sophie kindly. She propped a nearly finished portrait of Princess Poison on the easel. It showed Princess Poison's jet-black hair with its white streak tumbling down her shoulders, a haughty look on her face.

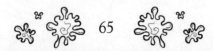

A necklace with a pendant shaped like a poison bottle gleamed around her neck.

"I ADORE it," said Princess Poison.

"What do you think?" Sophie asked Jinx, who was gazing at the portrait thoughtfully.

"Me?" Jinx asked nervously.

"Yes," said Sophie.

"Well …" said Jinx. "I don't think you've got the eyes quite right yet."

"Hmm," said Sophie, looking back and forth between Princess Poison and the portrait. "You're right. I haven't quite managed to capture the glint in them."

"The glint of evil," Charlotte muttered to Mia under her breath.

"Maybe you could add some flecks of white," Jinx suggested.

"Do you paint?" Sophie asked Jinx.

Jinx nodded. "I want to be an artist."

"Could you help me mix my paints?" Sophie asked her.

"I'd love to," said Jinx. "Is that OK?" she asked Princess Poison anxiously.

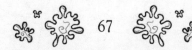

"If it means my portrait can be finished faster," Princess Poison said impatiently.

Jinx followed Sophie to the rear of the studio where there was a sink and a work surface covered with paints and paintbrushes.

"What are you doing here?" Princess Poison asked Mia and Charlotte. "Shouldn't you be off trying to grant that girl's silly wish?"

"It's not silly, and we are going to grant it," Mia said.

"And we're going to break the curse on Sophie too," Charlotte added defiantly.

"I very much doubt that," said Princess Poison.

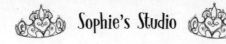

"We've broken the curse on three of the princesses' portraits," Charlotte said.

"Thanks to your meddling I've had to come up with an even more brilliant plan," Princess Poison said smugly. She pointed her wand at the painting. There was a flash

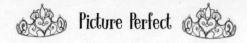

of green light and the unfinished portrait started to change. As the girls watched, another portrait appeared underneath it.

"That's Princess Sophie's self-portrait!" gasped Charlotte. It was one of the portraits that Princess Poison had cursed.

"Not any more," said Princess Poison gleefully. "Once Sophie has finished painting my portrait on top of it, all of her Secret Princess powers will be transferred to me. I will reclaim my rightful place at Wishing Star Palace and Sophie will be banished for ever!"

CHAPTER FIVE
Princess Poison's Plan

Mia and Charlotte stared at Princess Poison in horror.

"You can't do that!" Charlotte cried, feeling sick. The thought of Princess Poison stealing Princess Sophie's powers was unbearable.

"Oh yes I can," said Princess Poison. "And I have you to thank – I wouldn't have come

up with such an ingenious idea if you two hadn't wrecked my original plan!"

"Right," said Sophie, coming over with a palette of freshly mixed paints. "Are you ready to get started?"

"Ready as I'll ever be," said Princess Poison, tossing her hair and striking a pose.

"STOP!" yelled Mia. "Don't paint anything else! Look at the painting!"

Princess Poison pulled out her wand and aimed it at the canvas. It instantly became her unfinished portrait again.

"These children are very annoying," complained Princess Poison. "The paint fumes are making them imagine things. They should leave."

"It's an Open Day," Sophie said gently. "They can stay and watch." She dipped her paintbrush in black paint.

"We have to do something," Mia whispered urgently. "We can't let her finish the painting!"

Thinking fast, Charlotte said, "Can I take a closer look?" She walked towards the easel and pretended to trip. Flailing her arms

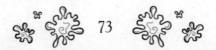

as she fell, she knocked the palette out of
Sophie's hand. It flew into the air and paint
splattered everywhere.

"Are you OK?"
Sophie asked.

Sophie was too kind
to be annoyed, but
Princess Poison was
furious. "I can't pose
with these little brats
around!" she shouted,
angrily wiping a blob
of paint off her nose.

"It was an accident," Sophie said.

"GET THEM OUT OF HERE!" growled
Princess Poison.

 74

"I'm so sorry, girls," said Sophie. "Would you mind leaving? I've still got quite a bit of work to do on this painting and you should probably get yourselves cleaned up."

Glancing down, Charlotte saw that she and Mia were covered in paint.

Reluctantly, the girls left Sophie's studio and walked back to Smart Arts feeling discouraged. Charlotte perked up when she saw a few customers chatting to Isla's mum inside the shop.

"What happened to you?" Isla asked them.

"It's a long story," Mia said, giving a sigh. "But the good news is that we managed to deliver all the fliers."

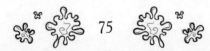

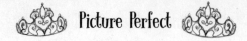

Isla helped the girls clean themselves up in the bathroom. "This will get the paint off," she said, pouring white spirit on a paper towel and scrubbing the girls' hands.

"Yuck!" said Charlotte. "It stinks!"

"Artists use it to clean their paintbrushes," said Isla.

The girls washed the white spirit off their hands and soon every trace of paint was gone.

"Thanks," said Mia.

"No," said Isla. "Thank you. Because the shop window looks so great, people have been coming into the shop."

As they emerged from the back room, the bell above the door jingled and another

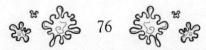

customer came in.

Charlotte groaned. It was Jinx!

"Can I help you?" Isla asked Jinx.

"I need to buy some oil paints," Jinx said. "For the artist Sophie Peters."

"I know Sophie's work," Isla's mum said, overhearing. "I'm a big fan."

"Me too," said Jinx.

"She has a funny way of showing it," Charlotte muttered to Mia.

"What should we do?" Mia whispered. "If Jinx buys more paint, Sophie will be able to finish Princess Poison's portrait."

"But if we're going to grant Isla's wish, the shop needs as many customers as possible," Charlotte whispered back. She bit her lip.

This was an impossible situation!

"Let's keep Jinx here for as long as possible," Mia said.

Jinx filled her shopping basket with paint and white spirit as she and Isla's mum chatted about art. The black and white cat meowed loudly and rubbed against Jinx's legs. "Don't mind Matisse," said Isla's mum. "He's just saying hello."

"Matisse is one of my favourite painters," said Jinx, patting the cat's head.

"What a nice big order," Isla's mum said happily. 'I'll bring this to the till and start ringing everything up," she added, taking the basket from Jinx.

"I'll help you, Mum," said Isla. "You can carry on looking around," she called over her shoulder.

"Yes," said Charlotte, hands on her hips. "Take all the time you want."

Jinx eyed Mia and Charlotte nervously. "Er, I don't need anything else."

She tried to step around the girls, but they blocked her way.

"How about a new easel?" said Charlotte.

"Or a new palette," said Mia, grabbing one from a table with a towering pyramid of

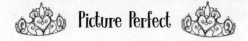
art and craft supplies.

Stepping backwards, Jinx bumped into the table. "Whoa!" she cried as the display toppled over.

CRASH! Pots of paint tumbled down, smashing and spilling on the floor. Skeins of yarn unravelled and beads scattered everywhere. Playfully pouncing on some wool, Matisse ran through a puddle of paint, tracking paw prints all over the carpet.

Picasso wanted to play too. Yowling, he jumped down from the table, knocking over a big container of glue. He ran through a pool of green paint, leaving a trail of green pawprints as he chased after Matisse.

Jinx tried to run away but her feet got

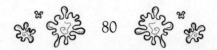

stuck in a puddle of spilled glue.

"Don't move!" Charlotte ordered, brandishing a ruler like a weapon.

"Why are you working for Princess Poison?" Mia demanded, pointing a glue gun at Jinx.

"Because it's the only way I'll get to be an artist!" wailed Jinx.

"Really?" said Charlotte sarcastically. "Helping Princess Poison spoil wishes is going to make you an artist?"

"That's not how it was supposed to be!" protested Jinx. "I made a wish to go to art school and Princess Poison said she'd grant it. She promised to get me a place at art school if I worked for her."

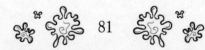

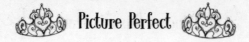

Tears rolling down her face, she continued. "At first I was really excited to be working at an art gallery. I didn't know anything about Secret Princesses and I didn't know that the Hexagon was just a nasty plan to hurt them. But by then it was too late – Princess Poison said she'd spoil my wish if I didn't follow her orders. I hate working for her, but I'll never be able to go to art school any other way."

Jinx lowered her head in shame.

Charlotte glanced at Mia. She could tell her tender-hearted friend felt sorry for Jinx.

"What if there was another way?" Mia said, thinking hard.

Jinx looked up hopefully.

"It's not your fault that Princess Poison tricked you," Mia said. "I know that Princess Sophie will want to grant your wish once she finds out about it. But we really need you to help us stop Princess Poison from stealing Sophie's powers."

"Why would Sophie help me after all the mean things I've done?" Jinx said.

"Because Secret Princesses are good and kind," said Mia. "They help people, not hurt them."

"What would I need to do?" Jinx asked them eagerly.

"Don't let Sophie finish Princess Poison's portrait," Charlotte said.

"So will you help us?" Mia asked.

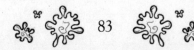

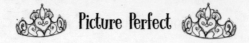

But before Jinx could answer, Hex burst into the shop and marched over to her. "There you are, slowcoach!" he said, sounding irritated. "You're keeping Princess Poison waiting. Hurry up and bring that paint to the studio."

Dashing to the counter, Jinx quickly paid for the paint. She followed Hex out of the shop, glancing over her shoulder at Mia and Charlotte as she left.

"Do you think she'll help?" Mia asked Charlotte.

"I don't know," said Charlotte. "But right now, Jinx is our only hope!"

CHAPTER SIX

A Stinky Spell

The shop's bell rang and a customer came in. It was a lady from the Old Warehouse.

"Hello," she said to Isla's mum. "I hear you sell beads."

Mia and Charlotte looked at the mess around them. Art supplies were strewn all over the floor. The cats had tracked paint and glue everywhere.

"She won't buy anything if she sees this,"
Mia said. "We'd better sort it out – fast!"

The girls put their pendants together.

"I wish the shop looked amazing," said Mia.

With a flash of light, the mess vanished.
Now paintbrushes dipped in different
colours hung upside-down from the ceiling,
forming a rainbow. Isla's origami birds hung

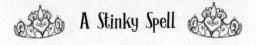
down from clear strings, as if they were
flying. Craft supplies had been arranged
to look like a waterfall. Felt and wool
tumbled down a cliff of paint pots and glue
containers with a pool of beads, buttons and
sequins at the bottom.

The magic had worked just in time. "Here
are our beads," said Isla's mum, leading the
lady to the craft aisle. Because of the magic,
Isla's mum didn't notice that the display
had been transformed, but Isla did.

"What did you do?" Isla whispered. "This
looks incredible."

"We used another wish," Mia said.

Before they could explain what had
happened, the shop bell rang again.

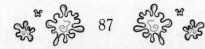

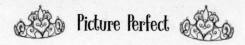

This time it was the potter. "I'd like to buy some clay," he told Isla.

Soon, the shop was full of customers. Many were artists the girls had met in their studios, but others had come in because of the pretty shop window. While her mother assisted customers, Isla went behind the counter to look after the till.

"This is amazing," said Isla. "We're almost too busy!"

"Maybe we could help?" suggested Mia. "We know where everything is now."

"That would be amazing," said Isla.

She handed the girls aprons that said *Smart Arts* and they slipped them on.

"Can I help you?" Charlotte asked a man

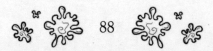

who had just entered the shop.

"I'd like to buy a gift for my daughter," he said. "She loves doing crafts."

As Charlotte helped the man pick a mosaic kit, Mia assisted an old lady who wanted wool to knit her new granddaughter a blanket.

Customers poured into Smart Arts and the girls helped them find what they needed.

"This is really fun," said Charlotte. She and her little brothers sometimes played shops at home, but working in a real shop was even better!

 89

Mia nodded. "I'm glad the shop is getting lots of customers," she said. "But I can't stop worrying about what's happening at the studio. What if Sophie finishes Princess Poison's portrait?"

"We just have to hope that Jinx believed that Sophie would help her," Charlotte said. "Do you think she will?"

"Jinx made a wish," said Mia. "It was just bad luck that Princess Poison got to her before a Secret Princess could. I'm sure Sophie will want to put that right."

The shop bell jingled again. Mia and Charlotte hurried to the entrance.

"Can I help y—" Charlotte stopped abruptly when she realised who the new

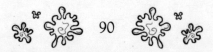

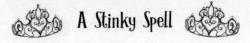
customer was – Princess Poison!

Has Sophie finished the painting?
Charlotte wondered, a rush of dread
flooding through her.

"Certainly," said Princess Poison. "You
can help me spoil someone's wish."

"We'd never do that!" Mia said.

"Is your portrait done?" Charlotte asked
apprehensively.

"Not yet – but soon, very soon," said
Princess Poison. "Sophie and Jinx are
mixing up the new paints so I thought I
would take a little walk." Glancing around
the shop disdainfully, Princess Poison
sneered, "It won't be hard to ruin Isla's wish.
This shop stinks."

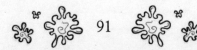

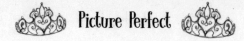
"No, it doesn't!" Mia said. "It's wonderful."

"Then I'll just have to *make* it stink," said Princess Poison. Pulling out her wand, she pointed it at Matisse and uttered a spell:

"Make this cat smell like a skunk,
Then this art shop will be sunk!"

Green light flew out of the wand and hit the black and white cat. *POOF!* He turned into a skunk.

"I'd better get back to the studio now," Princess Poison said, heading for the door. "My painting will soon be finished, then Wishing Star Palace, here I come!"

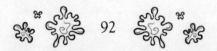

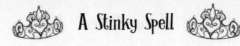

Mia and Charlotte stared at the skunk, which had black fur and two white stripes down its back.

"It's so cute," said Mia, who loved all animals. Holding out her hand, she stepped towards the skunk.

But Charlotte had seen skunks in California and knew what they did when they were scared.

"No, Mia!" she cried.

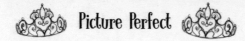

It was too late – the skunk lifted its bushy tail. *PPPPSSSSSSTTTTTT!* A horrible, stinky smell filled the shop.

"Ugh!" spluttered Mia, covering her nose. "That's disgusting!"

All around the shop, customers were coughing and holding their noses.

"What's that terrible smell?" asked the potter.

"Get me out of here!" gasped the old lady.

"Quick!" cried Charlotte. "We've got to do something or all the customers will leave."

Mia and Charlotte held their pendants together. They were glowing very faintly now, as there was only enough magic left

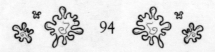

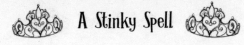

for one more wish.

"I wish for the shop to smell nice," said Charlotte.

"And for the skunk to turn back into Matisse," Mia added quickly.

FLASH! The skunk turned back into a cat, and a pleasant floral scent replaced the stinky odour. The customers returned to their shopping, instantly forgetting the bad smell.

"This is a great shop," said an artist waiting at the counter to pay for a sketchbook. "I can't believe I didn't know about it before, when it's so close to my studio. I'm going to get all of my supplies here from now on."

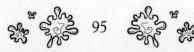

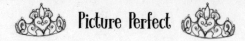

"Me too," said the artist behind her in the queue, who was holding a basket full of brushes and watercolours.

"Come again soon," Isla said to the potter, handing him a shopping bag.

"I will!" he said.

Once they had served every customer, Isla's mum shut the till's drawer and beamed. "We've done so well today," she said. "The customers all said they would come back. I think the shop is going to be a success after all!"

"That's great, Mum!" Isla said, giving her mother a big hug.

Suddenly the origami birds magically came to life and flew around the shop.

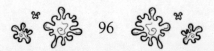

Paper swans, cranes and doves swooped and
fluttered overhead.

"We granted Isla's wish!" Mia said,
grinning at Charlotte.

Charlotte was really happy for Isla, but

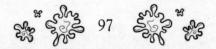

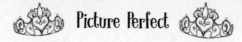
there was no time to celebrate. She took off her apron and handed it to Isla. "We've got to go now," she told her.

"Thank you so much for your help," Isla said. "Smart Arts is saved!"

"I'm sure it will do really well," said Mia.

Waving goodbye to Isla and her mother, Mia and Charlotte hurried out of the shop and sprinted towards the Old Warehouse.

"We've got to stop Sophie from finishing the painting," Charlotte said.

"And stop Princess Poison from stealing her powers!" said Mia.

There wasn't a moment to lose!

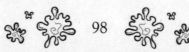

CHAPTER SEVEN
Jinx's Wish

"Hurry!" cried Charlotte, desperately hoping that they weren't too late.

They raced into the Old Warehouse and pounded up the stairs to Sophie's studio. Sophie was standing at her easel as Jinx cleaned paintbrushes. The fake smile on Princess Poison's face turned to a scowl when she spotted Mia and Charlotte.

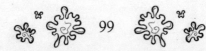

"We granted Isla's wish!" Charlotte announced triumphantly.

"You didn't stop us!" said Mia.

"That doesn't matter," said Princess Poison. "Because my portrait is done!"

"Well, not quite," said Sophie. "I just need to paint the streak in your hair."

"Get on with it then!" said Princess Poison.

"Don't!" cried Charlotte. "Please don't finish the painting! If you do, you'll stop being a Secret Princess."

"She'll steal all your powers," Mia said. "And you'll never be able to go back to Wishing Star Palace."

"I've told you girls," said Sophie patiently,

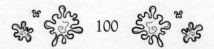

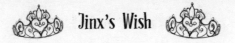

"I'm not a princess. I'm an artist." She dipped her paintbrush in white paint and raised it to the canvas.

"No!" yelled Charlotte. She charged at Sophie, intending to grab the paintbrush, but Jinx beat her to it.

SPLASH! Jinx threw a bottle of white spirit at the painting of Princess Poison. The paint remover dripped down the portrait, making the paint run.

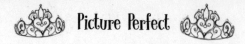
"You idiot!" shrieked Princess Poison.
"You stupid, clumsy girl!"

"My painting!" gasped Sophie. Green and
black paint streaked down the canvas.

"You'll never be an artist now!" Princess
Poison spat, glaring at Jinx. "You can kiss
your wish goodbye, Jinx!"

"My name isn't Jinx," Jinx shot back.
"It's Jessie! And even if my own wish never
comes true, I can't go on spoiling other
people's wishes!"

"You'll pay for this," Princess Poison said
menacingly. "Because I'm NEVER tired of
spoiling wishes!"

Sophie looked shocked to see how nasty
Princess Poison was being.

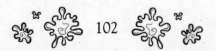

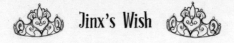

"Come back to Wishing Star Palace, Sophie!" begged Mia.

"You'll get your magic back and you can help Jinx," Charlotte said. "I mean, Jessie."

"I keep telling you girls – I'm not magic," Sophie said helplessly.

"Yes, you are!" insisted Mia. "You can paint magic pictures!"

"I wish I could!" said Sophie, staring at the ruined portrait.

Sparkling golden light streamed out of the paintbrush-shaped pendant on Sophie's necklace and hit the smeared portrait. Suddenly the image of Princess Poison started moving in the frame. Her toothy grin became a grimace as she tried to wipe

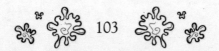

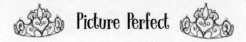
all the messy paint streaks off her dress.

"The painting is
… moving," said
Sophie, stunned.

"You're imagining
things," said Princess
Poison dismissively.

Sophie shook
her head. "I know
what I just saw.
It was magic."

Princess Poison grabbed her wand and
pointed it at Sophie threateningly. "Start
repainting my portrait before I get cross."

"No," said Sophie. "I … I think I believe
what the girls have been trying to tell me."

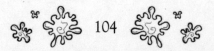

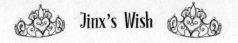

"This is all your fault," Princess Poison hissed at Jessie. "You're fired!" She waved her wand and a form appeared in her hand. "You won't be needing this any more!" Princess Poison tore the form in half.

"No!" cried Jessie. "That's my art school application form!"

Princess Poison ignored her, ripping Jessie's application into tiny pieces. Then she waved her wand and vanished in a flash of green light.

Jessie sank to her knees and stared at the scraps of her art school application strewn on the floor. "I worked so hard on that!"

"Do you really want to go to art school?" Sophie asked Jessie.

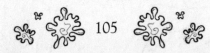

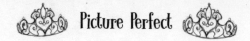

Jessie nodded. "But I'll never be able to go now."

"I wish I could help you, Jessie," said Sophie sadly.

There was a flash of light. The scraps of paper floated into the air and Jessie's art school application form was magically whole once more. Across it, in big red letters, was the word ACCEPTED.

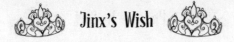

"You fixed my application form," Jessie said, amazed.

"I did?" said Sophie. Glancing down at the application form she was holding, Sophie said, "And it looks like you've got in. You're going to art school! "

Jessie looked happier than Mia and Charlotte had ever seen her. "This is incredible!" she said. "My wish is actually coming true!"

There was a burst of light and the ruined painting of Princess Poison faded, revealing Princess Sophie's portrait underneath it.

"That's me!" exclaimed Sophie, staring at her smiling face. "But why am I wearing a tiara?"

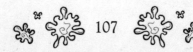

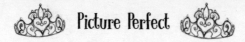

"You'll remember everything as soon as you go back to Wishing Star Palace," said Charlotte.

"Please come with us?" asked Mia.

Sophie hesitated.

"Could you look after the studio while I'm gone?" Sophie asked Jessie.

"Of course," Jesse replied. Turning to Mia and Charlotte, she said, "You told me that the Secret Princesses would help me and you were right. I'm so sorry for all the trouble I've caused."

"Everyone deserves a second chance," said Mia kindly.

"Just don't let Sophie down," Charlotte told her.

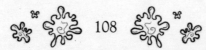

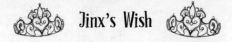
"I won't," Jessie assured them. "I promise."

Charlotte felt her feet tingle and looked down.

"Look, Mia!" she said. "The Secret Princesses have sent us our ruby slippers. Let's go!"

"Wait!" cried Mia. She ran over to the easel and tucked Sophie's self-portrait under her arm. "We can't forget this!"

Charlotte and Mia each took one of Sophie's hands. Clicking their heels together three times, they said, "Wishing Star Palace!"

A moment later, they were in a long corridor lined with paintings of Secret Princesses. Princess Sophie took her

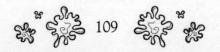

self-portrait out of Mia's hands and hung
it on the wall. "There!" she said, sighing
happily. "Back where it belongs, at Wishing
Star Palace! I remember everything now."

Sophie's painting hung near portraits
of Princess Cara, Princess Sylvie and
Princess Kiko. They had been cursed by
Princess Poison too, but thanks to Mia

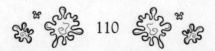

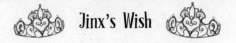
and Charlotte they were all safely back at Wishing Star Palace. Now there was only one blank space on the wall – where Princess Poison's portrait had once hung. And she was never coming back!

Mia shuddered. "I can't believe Princess Poison almost managed to steal your powers and come back to Wishing Star Palace."

"But she didn't," said Sophie. "Thanks to two amazing girls who broke her spell and made me believe in magic again." She smiled at Mia and Charlotte and took out her wand. "I can't wait to do some now." She pointed the wand first at Mia's necklace and then at Charlotte's. A blue sapphire appeared on both of their pendants.

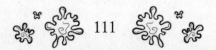

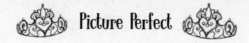

"That's your fourth sapphire!" said
Sophie. "Which means ..."
– she waved her wand
– "... you've earned
your princess rings!"

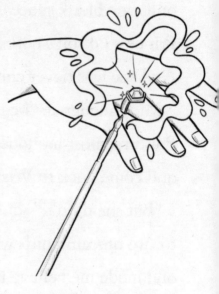

The four shining
sapphires disappeared
from Mia and
Charlotte's
heart-shaped
pendants, but now
they each had a sparkling sapphire ring on
their hand!

"Congratulations," Sophie said, hugging
them. "Come on, let's go and tell the others
the good news!"

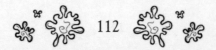

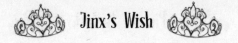
Outside Anna's bedroom, Charlotte put a finger to her lips. "Wait here," she whispered to Sophie. She and Mia entered the room. Princess Anna was still in bed, but she was looking a lot healthier. The other princesses were gathered around her bed, chatting.

"We brought you a surprise," said Charlotte.

Mia opened the door, and Princess Sophie walked in.

"Sophie!" the princesses cried joyfully.

"I'm back!" said Sophie. "Thanks to Mia and Charlotte."

"Your return isn't the only thing we have to celebrate," said Princess Anna, happily.

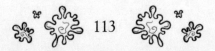

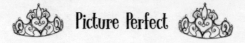

"I see that the girls have completed the third stage of their training."

The Secret Princesses crowded round to admire Mia and Charlotte's new rings.

"Our rings are gorgeous," said Mia. "But they'll look even better with our moonstone bracelets."

"When can we grant another wish?" Charlotte asked eagerly.

The princesses chuckled.

"I think you've granted enough wishes for one day," said Alice with a fond smile. "It's time for you two to go home."

Mia and Charlotte hugged each other goodbye.

"See you soon," Charlotte said.

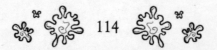

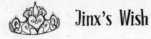

"To start earning moonstones!" Mia said, her eyes shining as bright as the jewels on their fingers. Alice waved her wand and, blinking, Charlotte found herself back in her bedroom.

"Quick, Charlotte, they're coming!" her dad called.

Charlotte ran to join him in the hallway. The front door opened and Liam and Harvey ran into the house.

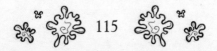

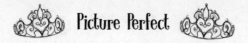

"Whoa!" said Liam, noticing the balloons.

"Cool!" cried Harvey, pointing at the birthday banner.

"Surprise!" everyone shouted.

"Let me take a picture," Charlotte's mum said, posing everyone underneath the banner. Setting the timer on her camera, she ran to get into the picture.

FLASH!

"Aw," said Charlotte's mum, checking how the picture had come out. "What a lovely family portrait."

Glowing with pride, Charlotte thought about another portrait – the one she and Mia had saved today. They had broken Princess Poison's curse and earned their

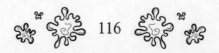

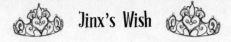
sapphire rings, bringing them one step
closer to becoming Secret Princesses.
Hopefully their own portraits would hang
at Wishing Star Palace one day – and
Charlotte couldn't think of anything better!

The End

Join Charlotte and Mia in their next Secret Princesses adventure, Ballet Dream!

Read on for a sneak peek!

Ballet Dream

"Found it!" called Charlotte Williams, trying to tug a large plastic box out from where it was wedged between a bag of golf clubs, two surf boards and a tent.

"Let me give you a hand," said Charlotte's dad, helping her drag the box of Christmas decorations out. Mopping his brow, he gazed around their garage, which was jam-packed with sports equipment, gardening tools and beach toys. "I have no idea how we've managed to get so much stuff so quickly!" he said.

Charlotte's family hadn't lived in California for very long, but they loved it – especially the hot weather. When they weren't at work or at school, they were usually outdoors having fun in the sun.

Charlotte and her dad carried the box into the front garden, where her mum was watering the plants and her twin brothers, Liam and Harvey, were playing catch.

"Who wants to help put up the Christmas lights?" called Charlotte, tucking her brown curls behind her ears.

Charlotte and her dad wound a string of fairy lights around a palm tree.

"Look!" cried Liam. He pulled out a light-up reindeer. "I found Rudolph!"

Harvey held up a snowman decoration. "And here's Frosty the Snowman!"

"Hey, what do snowmen eat for breakfast," Charlotte asked the twins. Without waiting for them to reply, she said, "Frosted flakes!"

Read Ballet Dream
to find out what
happens next!

Isla's Origami Twirling Bird

This little bird would look lovely hanging in your bedroom, or would make a cute gift for someone! Use coloured paper to make it look even prettier.

Steps

1) Start with a square piece of paper. Fold it in half diagonally, so one corner touches the corner opposite and it makes a triangle.

2) Fold it in half again to make another, smaller triangle, then open it up to how it looked in step 1. This will make a crease so that folding is easier.

3) Fold the top corner down so that it pokes over the bottom edge, then fold the model in half again corner to corner so that the sides match up.

4) Turn the model so that it points upwards.

5) Fold down both of the top flaps.

6) Then fold the wings back up as shown.

7) Your bird is complete! Give it a twirl and watch it fly.

Famous Artists

Matisse and Picasso aren't just the cutest
cats ever, they were named after two
amazing artists who happened to be BFFs!

Matisse

- Matisse discovered he loved art when he was ill as a child and his mother gave him some art supplies to stop him getting bored!
- He experimented with many different art forms including landscapes and still life.
- He founded the art movement 'Fauvism' which means 'Wild Beasts' and involves painting a lot of bright colours freely to show emotions.
- He also made a lot of big paper collages which he called "painting with scissors".

Picasso

- His full name is 23 words long!
- The first word he said was "pencil".
- He made his first painting at the age of nine.
- He helped to found the art movement of Cubism, which means painting in the style of a lot of little cubes.
- Matisse was his best friend.

♥ WIN A PRINCESS GOODY BAG ♥

Secret PRINCESSES
What would you wish for?

Design your own dress and win a Secret Princesses goody bag for you and your best friend!

Charlotte and Mia get to wear beautiful dresses at Wishing Star Palace, but now they want you to design one for them.

To enter all you have to do is follow these steps:

Go to **www.secretprincessesbooks.co.uk**

♥ Click the competition module
♥ Download and print the activity sheet
♥ Design a beautiful dress for Charlotte or Mia
♥ Send your entry to:

Secret Princesses: The Sapphire Collection Competition
Hachette Children's Group
Carmelite House
50 Victoria Embankment
London
EC4Y 0DZ

Closing date: 2nd December 2017

For full terms and conditions,
www.hachettechildrens.co.uk/
TermsandConditions/secretprincessesdresscompetition.page

Good luck!

Secret PRINCESSES

What would you wish for?

Lots of fun activities

Monthly treasure hunt

Create a secret profile

Earn princess points

Join in the fun at secretprincessesbooks.com

Secret
PRINCESSES

What would you wish for?

Are you a Secret Princess?

Join the Secret Princesses Club at:

secretprincessesbooks.co.uk

Explore the magic of the
Secret Princesses and discover:

♥ Special competitions! ♥
♥ Exclusive content! ♥
♥ All the latest princess news! ♥

Open to UK and Republic of Ireland residents only
Please ask your parent/guardian for their permission to join

For full terms and conditions go to
secretprincessesbooks.co.uk/terms

Sapphire14

Enter the special code above on the website to receive

50 Princess Points